...This...

and my three best friends
– Haggis, Fiend and Norman.
They're monsters.

That's right. **Monsters**. Big hairy
critters with fangs and horns
and extra eyes.

They were living in the basement of
the house my family moved into.
Don't tell anyone, will you?
They're a secret. Only me, my parents
and my big sister Angela
know about them...

*With special thanks to
Richard Dungworth*

For more monster mess and chaos,
try reading:
Me & My Monsters: Monsters in the Basement
Me & My Monsters: Monster Mess

Based on a script entitled
Monster Smart by
Mark Huckerby and Nick Ostler

Me and My Monsters is co-created by
Mark Grant and Claudia Lloyd

Me & My MONSTERS™

Monster School!

RORY GROWLER

PUFFIN

PUFFIN BOOKS

Published by the Penguin Group
Penguin Books Ltd, 80 Strand, London WC2R 0RL, England
Penguin Group (USA) Inc., 375 Hudson Street, New York, New York 10014, USA
Penguin Group (Canada), 90 Eglinton Avenue East,
Suite 700, Toronto, Ontario, Canada M4P 2Y3
(a division of Pearson Penguin Canada Inc.)
Penguin Ireland, 25 St Stephen's Green, Dublin 2, Ireland
(a division of Penguin Books Ltd)
Penguin Group (Australia), 250 Camberwell Road, Camberwell, Victoria 3124, Australia
(a division of Pearson Australia Group Pty Ltd)
Penguin Books India Pvt Ltd, 11 Community Centre,
Panchsheel Park, New Delhi – 110 017, India
Penguin Group (NZ), 67 Apollo Drive, Rosedale, Auckland 0632, New Zealand
(a division of Pearson New Zealand Ltd)
Penguin Books (South Africa) (Pty) Ltd, 24 Sturdee Avenue,
Rosebank, Johannesburg 2196, South Africa

Penguin Books Ltd, Registered Offices: 80 Strand, London WC2R 0RL, England

puffinbooks.com

First published 2011
001 – 10 9 8 7 6 5 4 3 2 1

Copyright © Tiger Aspect Productions/The Jim Henson Company/Sticky Pictures Pty Ltd 2011
Me & My Monsters ™ & © Tiger Aspect Productions/The Jim Henson Company/
Sticky Pictures Pty Ltd 2011.
Me & My Monsters is produced by Tiger Aspect Productions, The Jim Henson Company
and Sticky Pictures Pty Ltd.
All rights reserved

Set in Futura Standard
Printed in Great Britain by Clays Ltd, St Ives plc

British Library Cataloguing in Publication Data
A CIP catalogue record for this book is available from the British Library

ISBN: 978-0-141-33669-5

www.greenpenguin.co.uk

MIX
Paper from
responsible sources
FSC
www.fsc.org   FSC™ C018179

Penguin Books is committed to a sustainable
future for our business, our readers and our
planet. This book is made from paper certified
by the Forest Stewardship Council.

Trouble

I've been called a lot of things in
my life. As well as Eddie, I mean.

'Messy' is one of Mum's favourites.
I get that a lot. And Dad calls me
'clumsy' pretty often. As for what
my adorable (not) big sister Angela
calls me – well, she usually goes
for maximum nastiness.

'Eddie! You're *disgusting*!'

See what I mean? All
because, sometimes, I like to treat
her to a close-up view of my mouth
when I'm eating. (For me, it's the
highlight of family mealtimes.)

But 'smart'? That's not a label I've had to worry about. Since we moved in with the monsters, school's been the last thing on my mind. When you've got Fiend, Haggis and Norman to hang out with, school stuff tends to drop off the bottom of your Things To Do list.

Mind you, I was beginning to worry now. It was Report Time. My least favourite part of the school year.

Angela's school report had come in the morning's post, which meant mine was on its way, too. And with the amount of work I'd been putting in lately – or rather *hadn't* been putting in – it wasn't

6

going to make impressive reading.
If my grades were as bad as I was
expecting them to be, Mum and Dad
were going to toast me.

I may not get called 'smart' very
often, but I'm smart enough to know
when I'm in trouble.

A is for Angela
(and Annoying)

A

For now, at least, my parents were concentrating on my sister's report. Dad was reading it at the breakfast table.

A

'I'm seeing a lot of pointy letters here!' he crowed. 'Not curvy C's! Not bendy B's!'

No surprises there. Angela has been a straight A student for as long as I can remember. She's annoyingly brainy. But to be fair, my sister looked like she was finding Dad's cringe-worthy reaction to her grades as painful as I was.

A

A

A
A

'Why don't you speak like a normal person?' she said, scowling at him.

Mum gave Dad a look, too. 'You're embarrassing Angela,' she told him.

But Dad wasn't bothered. Embarrassing us is what he does best.

'I'm talking an *Ay*-valanche of *Ay*-cademic *Ay*-ccomplishments!' he cried.

Groan.

'Now you're just embarrassing *yourself*,' said Mum.

A

'Ah, come on!' Dad protested. 'Why can't I be proud of my brainy little princess?'

A

Angela squirmed. 'Brainy little princess' isn't exactly the image she's been working on.

A

'Oh, give it up, Dad!' she wailed. 'Anyway, those grades only went and got me extra homework to "stretch" me.' She pulled a face. 'So it turns out being smart *isn't* so smart.'

Extra homework? I shivered. That was just plain evil.

But Dad still didn't let up. 'Oh, I'm sure you'll *Ay*-ce it!' he told her, beaming.

A

'Can we change the subject?' Angela pleaded.

A

Thank goodness for that.

'Maybe there's somebody else at this table with a school report due?' she said, giving me a sly look.

What? Oh, thanks a *lot*, sis. Drop me right in it, why don't you?

A

But I wasn't going to be cornered
so easily. It was time for evasive
action . . .

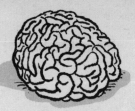

Brains in the Family

'Ooh! I have a question!' I said, quickly trying to think of one that would divert my parents' attention from the subject of my report. 'Where does Angela get her brains from?'

With any luck, my parents would be only too happy to talk about themselves for a while. They usually were.

'*Well . . .*' began Mum, looking rather pleased with herself. I could tell she was searching for a way to say 'from me', without sounding like a fathead. But Dad got in first.

'Guilty as charged!' he said

proudly. The fat-head thing doesn't
bother Dad so much.

'Ha!' Mum glared at him and
snorted. She obviously thought it was
a bit rich for Dad to claim that *he* had
passed on the brainbox gene.

But Dad saw things differently. He
gave Mum a patronizing smile. 'Look,
you may be a wonderful, talented
woman, my sweetness,' he told her,
'but *I* am the one who came top of his
class in college.'

Mum gave another snort. 'Your
degree was in *surfing*!'

'Surf *science*, remember,' Dad
corrected her. 'That's completely
different.'

Mum didn't look convinced.

'Well, I read English, at a proper
university,' she said.

Dad wasn't impressed. 'It doesn't
sound as clever as "science", though,
does it? I mean *anyone* can read
English . . .'

So far, my plan was working like
a dream. My parents were too busy
squabbling over who was the smartest

to ask about my report. But just as I thought I was out of danger, Mum broke off their argument. She gave me one of her looks.

'Eddie,' she said. 'Is there any reason we should be worried about *your* school report?'

A whole bunch of reasons. My grades, for one thing. And my teachers' comments for another. But I wasn't about to say so. I smiled at Mum, hoping her X-ray mother-vision wouldn't see right through me.

'Let's just say I'm . . .'

Desperately worried. Expecting the worst. As good as dead.

'. . . quietly confident,' I lied.

Desperate Plans

'**I'm completely dead!**'

I flopped on to the monsters' sofa, downstairs in their basement den. The guys all crowded round looking worried.

'What's wrong?' asked Haggis.

Norman gave a concerned '**BRROO-DLOOP?**'

'Eddie's brain must be overheating,' said Fiend. 'If we don't do something, it'll boil like an egg and explode out of his ears like a . . . big . . . explodey . . . eary . . . thing!'

Suddenly, a jet of freezing cold water hit me on the side of the head.

It soaked my hair and face, and ran down the back of my neck. I yelled and leapt off the sofa to get out of the way. 'Hey!'

Norman had just squirted a soda fountain of cold water at me, fire-extinguisher style. I guess he was trying to cool down my about-to-explode brain, after Dr Fiend's diagnosis. All three of them were looking at me like they'd just saved my life.

'No need to thank us,' Fiend told me. 'We are here to serve.'

I grabbed a towel to dry off and decided to share what was on my mind – before they could give me any more emergency medical treatment.

'This is serious, guys! My school report could arrive any minute.'

'**School?**' Fiend pulled a face. (Not hard when you've got nine eyes.) 'Pah! I don't understand what you do at that place all day!' Nor did I, I thought to myself. That was the problem.

'Besides,' Fiend went on, 'you learn all the important stuff from us. Do they ever teach you *this* at that so-called "school" of yours?'

He let rip with several seconds'

worth of impressive belching. Fiend's
burps are pretty special. He can
change their pitch, like he's playing
an instrument. Haggis joined in with
a bubbling tummy-rumble baseline
and Norman yodelled over the top.
The combined sound was . . . **unusual**.
A bit rude-sounding maybe. But
definitely impressive.

I agreed with Fiend. Monster burping was way better than times tables or handwriting practice. But it wouldn't help get me out of my current crisis. There was a report full of F grades heading my parents' way and I needed to stop it.

'You know who Mum and Dad will blame, don't you?' I said.

Fiend took a wild guess.

'Themselves?'

'No!' I replied. '**YOU!** Because I spend all my time playing down here when I should be upstairs studying.'

All three of them looked a little puzzled. They often found themselves on the wrong side of my parents, but had never quite figured out why. I knew

20

why, of course. Mum and Dad were grown-ups. Enough said.

'There's only one thing left to do,' I said.

Fiend nodded enthusiastically. 'Let's torch the place and blame it on a meteor shower!' Hmmm. Not *quite* what I'd had in mind.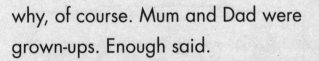

'*No*,' I told him. 'We have to get to that report, before my parents do.'

Fiend looked disappointed. 'OK,' he grumbled. 'We'll try *your* idea first.'

There wasn't a moment to lose. If we were to intercept my report, we needed a detailed mission plan. Fast.

It was time for

OPERATION POST STOP.

Operation Post Stop

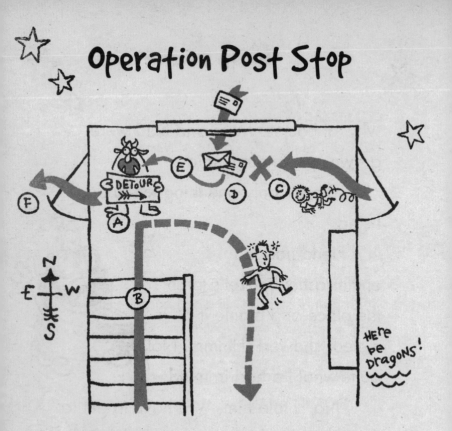

OBJECTIVE: To intercept the morning post and prevent any letters from school reaching the enemy (my parents).

TIME FRAME: Early tomorrow morning, in time for the postman's delivery.

OPERATIVES:
* Agent E. Carlson
* Agent Haggis

EQUIPMENT:

* 'DETOUR' roadworks sign from Norman's collection (For Agent Haggis).
* Full-body camouflage (for me Agent Carlson)

ACTION PLAN:

* (A) Haggis to station himself at foot of stairs with detour sign. Sign will direct enemy agent (Dad) past front door without stopping. (B) (Enemy should be in usual zonked-out, gormless, just-woken-up state, so unlikely to notice anything suspicious.)

* (C) When enemy has cleared the area, Agent Carlson to commando-roll from dining room and assume position beside doormat. (D)

* When post delivered, Agent Carlson to seize all letters and place them in Agent Haggis's mouth for swallowing. (E)

* Both agents to return immediately to basement HQ for analysis of intercepted post. (F)

Haggis Brings Something Up

The operation went like clockwork. Not a single hitch. Only seconds after we had swiped the post from the hallway, me and Haggis were safely down in the basement with Fiend and Norman. And the enemy – sorry, my parents – were none the wiser. Now all we had to do was check whether our haul included my school report. This was going to be the messy bit.

I quickly pulled on my waterproof mac and snapped my swimming goggles over my eyes. Then I turned to

Norman. 'OK, Norm.'

I took a deep breath. **'Do it.'**

Norman was standing at Haggis's left side. At my signal, he made a high-pitched warbling sound. Haggis opened his mouth wide. Norman lifted Haggis's arm as high as he could. Then he swung it firmly back down, like a huge hairy pump lever.

A great gloopy mass of slime-covered stuff erupted from Haggis's massive monster mouth and splattered on to the basement floor. The letters he'd swallowed a few minutes earlier were the first things to come flooding out. But that wasn't all.

The contents of Haggis's stomach

landed at my feet. *Ew*. There was a
remote-controlled car in there. And
a number plate. An entire ball of
wool, too. And Mum's kitchen sieve.
Everything was coated with sticky
monster tummy-gunk. Yuck.

But Haggis hadn't finished yet.
'Oooh! Oooh! Wait!' he cried. He
coughed a couple of times before he
could explain. 'Furball!'

I quickly stepped back. There was another splatter, followed by a terrified

'MIIAAOOOOOW!'

I caught sight of a small soggy-looking animal before it dashed for cover.

Haggis looked rather embarrassed. 'Oh,' he said bashfully. 'I don't know where *that* came from.' Only Haggis could accidentally swallow a cat.

Thankfully, that was the lot. At least, I hoped so. I knelt down to take a closer look at the slimy pile. **Eeuurgh!**

It was time to check the post.

Reasons to be Smart

I went through the pile of slimy envelopes one more time.

Rats. 'I don't believe this,' I told the guys.

'THE REPORT ISN'T HERE!'

I'd been *sure* it would arrive that morning. But it hadn't. Which meant that the whole operation had been a waste of time. We'd gone to all that trouble and my report could still drop on the doormat in the next post. I was no nearer to keeping it away from my parents than before.

I took off my goggles and slumped

down on the monsters' sofa again, properly fed-up. 'We're going to need an *extra* clever plan for tomorrow,' I groaned. Haggis and Norman started making little grunting noises and pulling faces as they tried to think. But Fiend couldn't see the point.

'I don't get it,' he said. 'What's the big deal with being *smart* anyway?'

'*I* don't know,' I told Fiend. 'It's like, if you're intelligent, then people respect you more.'

Fiend's expression brightened. 'So – if we were smarter, then maybe your mum and dad would like *us* more?' he said. 'And do really nice things, like . . . pat us on the head?'

29

Haggis's eyes lit up. 'Or feed us *shoes*!' he said dreamily.

'Yeah!' Fiend went on excitedly. 'And finally let me take that ride in the washing machine!'

Norman had his own plans for how my parents might reward him. He let out a series of squeals, gurgles and **wooo-heeee!** noises.

Fiend frowned at him, shaking his head. 'Norman,' he said. 'No one in their right mind is going to let you do *that* in their refrigerator.'

Norman gave a small disappointed hoot. I couldn't help wondering what he'd been hoping for.

'So,' muttered Fiend to himself, 'if we want to get some love, we've got to get some *brains* . . .' Then, for once, he was quiet for a moment or two.

I should have seen the warning signs. Fiend only ever shuts up when his monster mind has gone into overdrive thinking up one of his (not so) brilliant ideas. But right then, I was too busy with my own ideas to wonder what Fiend was plotting. I *had* to come up with another plan to intercept my school report. I decided the basement perhaps wasn't the best place to concentrate – mainly because the pile of junk from Haggis's stomach was beginning to whiff a bit.

Brain buzzing, I headed upstairs to my room, to work on Plan B.

The Brainiest Grown-up

Coming up with brilliant plans is hard work. After about half an hour of serious brainstorming up in my room, I was ready for some idea-boosting snacks. I went down to the kitchen to help myself. Unfortunately, my parents were in there. Dad was waving his newspaper at Mum.

'There! *I've* just finished the *extra hard* crossword!' he boasted. 'All by myself. I guess that makes *me* one of the top two per cent of brains in the world who can do that kind of thing.'

Mum didn't look that impressed. 'Maybe in a world where flubberifically is an actual word,' she said, frowning.

It looked like they were still arguing over who was the smartest. Mum and Dad can really drag out stuff like that. There was no way *I* wanted to get involved. I decided to grab whatever snacks I could and make a swift exit.

But just then, Mum opened a kitchen cupboard to get something – and gave a little scream. I could see Fiend crouching inside.

'FIEND!' cried Mum. 'You scared me! You're not making another stinky nest again, are you?'

I really hoped not. I found the last one in the laundry basket. It wasn't nice.

'No,' said Fiend. 'I was just reading, thinking, being *smart* in a generally *smart* kind of *smarty*-pants way.' He pointed to the stuff on the shelf beside him. 'These are some *great* books.'

Mum pointed out the obvious. 'Those are cereal boxes.'

'And they are a *gripping* read,' said Fiend.

The next moment, Haggis came lumbering into the kitchen, clutching a toilet roll. He was holding it up to one eye and chuckling happily.

'I found *this* interesting book in the little smelly room,' he told us all proudly. He let the toilet paper unroll, as though it was the best trick ever. **'Ta-da! It's very clever.'**

Dad shook his head. 'What scares me the most,' he muttered, 'is that I'm actually getting used to this kind of thing now.'

I knew what he meant. But there was something *particularly* odd about today's dose of monster nonsense. Since when had Fiend and Haggis been interested in *books*?

Before I could ask them, Angela burst through the door. Norman was with her. They were wrestling over one of my sister's school textbooks.

Norman had his teeth sunk deep into it and was refusing to let go.

'**NORMAN!**' Angela yelled at him.

'I am not teaching you algebra!'

That was enough for Mum. 'All right, what's going on?' she said to the monsters. 'Come on, out with it.'

Fiend gave a sigh. 'OK, I'll level with you,' he said sadly. **'We're idiots.'**

'What? No!' Mum tried to be generous. 'No, of course not!' I saw Angela give her a look.

'Well . . . a *little* bit maybe,' Mum admitted.

'So we were thinking you guys could teach us all that reading and writing stuff,' said Fiend hopefully.

'You know – make us smarter.'

So *that* was what it was all about!
The penny dropped. After what I'd told
the guys down in the basement – about
how being smart could make people
think more of you – they were trying to
improve their monster minds!

Dad let out a howl of hysterical
laughter, then looked Fiend straight in
the eyes. Or some of them anyway.
'No,' he said flatly.

Poor old Haggis. He doesn't handle
rejection well. Dad turning him and
Fiend down was too much. He burst

into tears, the big softy.
'Oh, Haggis!
No, shush now . . .'
said Angela.

38

I nearly had to pinch myself.
Angela was trying to comfort Haggis.
My sister, the ice queen, feeling sorry
for someone.

'You wouldn't want *Dad* to teach
you anyway,' she told Haggis. 'Believe
me.' She had a point. Dad's teaching
style is the *worst*.

Dad gave Angela an offended
look. 'Ahh, come on!' he protested.
'Who taught you to count before you
were a year old? You remember the
Number Song?'

Oh, yes. We both remember it.

'Dad, your songs gave me and
Eddie **nightmares**,' Angela reminded
him. 'Remember? We had to have
counselling.'

Mum sniggered. Dad turned on her. 'You can laugh all you want, little Miss Smarty-pants,' he told her, 'but *I* could teach mathematics to a complete **numbskull!**'

At this, Haggis and Fiend suddenly perked up. '*We're* numbskulls!' cried Haggis.

'**BING–BING!**' agreed Norman enthusiastically.

'**Teach us!**

Teach us!' shrieked Fiend.

Mum must have seen an opportunity to get one over on Dad. She gave him a hard stare. 'All right, Mr Surf Science,' she said. 'The first to teach one of the monsters something useful is the undisputed brainiest grown-up. *Deal?'*

Dad was too proud to back down now. He took Mum's outstretched hand and shook it firmly. 'Deal,' he said.

What are they like? They'll compete over *anything*. Sometimes, I wonder what it would be like to have grown-up parents, like other kids . . .

The moment Dad accepted Mum's challenge, the monsters began making an absolute racket.

'Pick me! Pick me!' cried Fiend.

'Pick me! I want to be picked!' boomed Haggis.

41

'**BOO-BOO-DRRRING!**' yodelled Norman.

Funny, isn't it? I'd do more or less anything to get out of school. But here were Fiend, Haggis and Norman pestering my parents to teach them. You never can tell with monsters.

Mum looked undecided for a moment. Then she made her choice. 'Fiend!'

'**Yeah!**' whooped Fiend. 'Ha ha!'

'All right,' agreed Dad. 'I'll take Haggis.'

Haggis looked like he was going to burst with excitement. '**Oh! Yes! Yes!**'

I saw Norman look at Angela hopefully. But that wasn't going to happen. Not in a million years.

'Absolutely *no* way,' she told
Norman firmly. To underline the fact
that she wanted no part in Mum and
Dad's ridiculous contest, she headed
back to her room.

It suddenly struck me that I needed
to do the same. For a while there,
I'd forgotten about the School Report
Situation. I'd been down here too long
already. If I was to stop that dreaded
document falling into my parents'
hands, I needed to get back to my
mission plan . . .

Where Did Everybody Go?

After another tough session at my bedroom desk, I reckoned I'd cracked it. I finally had what I needed. A cunning plan to intercept the next morning's post. It was a pretty cool plan, too. I was rather proud of it. Particularly the bit where my fishing rod and unicycle came in.

By the time I'd worked out the last few vital details, my desk was covered with location diagrams, mission schedules and equipment lists. I took down my pinboard and stuck all my sketches and notes to it. Then I carried the whole lot down to the basement.

It was time to brief the guys on Phase Two of Operation Post Stop.

'OK, listen up, men,' I said as I came down the bottom steps. 'That report *has* to arrive tomorrow. So let's make the next operation our best yet. I'm sure if we all pull our weight, we'll . . .' But nobody was listening. There wasn't a monster in sight.

'FIEND? HAGGIS? NORM?'

No reply. The place was deserted.

Where were they all? Still up in the kitchen? Mum would have told them to clear out by now, surely? Didn't they realize we had a vital mission to rehearse? Then I remembered Mum and Dad's teach-a-numbskull contest.

Maybe the guys were already having their first lessons.

I put down my pinboard and headed back upstairs. I had to find out whether I could still count on my monster mission team – or whether I'd be tackling Phase Two alone . . .

A Lesson for Haggis...

I guess I shouldn't have been surprised that my parents had started teaching their monster students straight away. When they made that deal, they meant business. You know how competitive most grown-ups can get? Well, mine are like that, times a hundred. The monsters had no idea what they'd let themselves in for.

From the hall, I could hear voices coming from Dad's study. I tiptoed over and silently peered round the door to see what was going on. Oh, no. No way.

Dad had really gone to town on

the teacher thing. He had even dug
out his old Number Dungas – these
embarrassing red dungarees with
numbers stitched all over them. He
used to wear them whenever he tried to
teach me and Angela maths, when we
were little.

He was standing in front of Haggis
holding up two battered old hand-
puppets. I recognized them, too. Dad
had made them to help teach me and
my sister to count. All they actually
did was give us both nightmares. Dad
calls the cardboard-box robot one
Geometron. The other one, a papier-
mâché professor, is Alge-Brian. I know
– sad, isn't it? Dad really likes doing
their voices, too. Badly. Right now he

was waggling them about as though
they were talking to one another.

'Hello, Geometron,' said Dad,
trying to sound professory. 'Are you
going to teach me about numbers?'
More waggling of the robot puppet.

'Affirmative, Alge-Brian!' Dad's
robot voice is particularly rubbish.
'Numbers are fun-fun-fun! One . . . two
. . . three . . . four . . . five . . .'

Poor Haggis was watching in
wide-eyed horror. His eyes were glued
to the puppets' every move. He began
slowly backing away, towards the
study wall. I could see the puppets
were really freaking him out. Tell me
about it, Hag.

Dad ploughed on with the lesson,

49

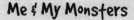

oblivious. '*Six . . . seven . . . eight
. . . nine . . . ten,*' whined Geometron.
'*Now you have a turn, Haggis!*' Dad
held the robot puppet up in front of
Haggis, as though it was speaking
to him. Its cardboard head suddenly
flopped sideways and fell off.

This was too much for Haggis.
'ARRRRRGGHHH!' he wailed, eyes
wider than ever.

Dad tried to calm him down. 'Haggis, Haggis . . . Remember what I said? About the puppets not being real?'

Haggis wasn't having any of it. 'But . . . but I heard them **talking!**'

Dad, always at his best when it comes to getting it completely wrong, waggled the professor puppet in front of Haggis's petrified face. *'Don't be scared, Haggis!'* he said in his special Alge-Brian voice.

One of the puppet's papier-mâché eyes suddenly popped right out. That was it. Haggis snapped. I flattened myself against the wall as he came charging past into the hallway, screaming his monster lungs out.

'AAAARRRRRRRRRRGGGGGHHHHHH!'

From what I'd seen, I couldn't imagine Haggis getting through his counting lesson any time soon. But perhaps Fiend would still be free to help with Phase Two. I decided to go and check on him and Mum, to see if his lesson was going any more smoothly than Haggis's . . .

...And a Lesson for Fiend

Mum was giving Fiend his first lesson
in the kitchen. I peered round the
door, trying not to disturb them. Fiend
was perched on the kitchen worktop,
listening to Mum.

'OK, Fiend,' said Mum
enthusiastically. 'Let's see what you've
got. Name three countries for me.'

'Easy!' said Fiend,
looking pleased. 'Er . . .
Basement Land . . .
Sitting-Roomania . . .
and . . .' I could see
he was struggling to
come up with a third.

'And Ant World!'

Mum gave him a puzzled look. 'Ant World?'

'Yeah.' Fiend looked at Mum like she was a real thicko. 'Where all the ants live. Duh.'

I could see how Fiend's monster logic was working, but I was pretty sure Ant World wasn't in *my* geography textbook.

'**Hmmmm ...**' said Mum. 'Maybe we should try something a little less ambitious.' She moved towards the fridge. 'Something . . . easier for you to digest.'

'Aahh,' said Fiend. 'You mean like your sheepskin slippers?'

Mum had her head in the fridge and must have only half heard. 'My what?' she called.

'Oh, er, nothing!' Fiend said quickly. 'Anyway,' he muttered to himself, 'that was weeks ago. And you didn't even notice.' I rolled my eyes and left them to it.

Going Solo

The clock was ticking. I needed to move on with my scheme to intercept my school report. And it was clear that for once, I couldn't bank on the monsters' help. From what I'd seen, Fiend and Haggis were going to be tied up with lessons from Mum and Dad for a long time yet. But monsters or no monsters, the mission must go on.

One good thing about my parents being obsessed with their contest was that they weren't paying any attention to me. It was a cinch to gather up the kit I needed – my rod, unicycle and all the other stuff – and sneak down to the hallway with it.

It was well past my bedtime. Normally, Mum and Dad would have had something to say about me even coming downstairs so late, let alone setting up camp by the front door for the night. But they were far too busy teaching the monsters to notice. So I took up my planned position, set up my equipment and began the long wait for the early morning postal delivery.

Doormats are *really* prickly, aren't they? As I shuffled about, trying to get comfortable for my overnight stake-out at the front door, I could hear Teacher Mum and Teacher Dad battling on with their struggling students. From what

I could overhear from Dad's study, it
sounded like Haggis was still having
a tough time getting to grips with
numbers . . .

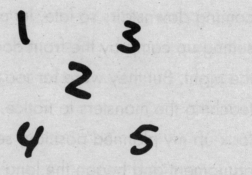

A Lesson for Haggis
(continued)

'See, Haggis?' Dad was saying. 'The puppets are gone, OK? I promise.'
He was obviously still trying to calm Haggis down after the popping-eyeball incident.

'We'll try something else, all right?' Dad went on encouragingly. 'Are you ready? I might be a bit rusty, but . . .'
I cringed at the sound of Dad breaking into song.

'one is the number that we're starting with!'

No. Not the Number Song.
Anything but that. Poor Haggis.

'Two is the number that
comes after one!'

I could imagine Dad dancing about
in front of Haggis, waving his hands in
the air. The man has no shame.

'Three is the number after
the next one,
which remember was two not one.
And then there's ...'

The memories were flooding back.
No amount of counselling could
erase them.

'Four is the number that
comes after three,
Numbers are so ee-ea-sy!
Numbers are just so much fun,
come on, Haggis, and sing along!'

Despite Dad's encouragement, I couldn't hear any evidence of Haggis joining in. After a while Dad's singing trailed off pathetically. Then I heard someone sobbing. Human sobs, not monster ones. Dad had obviously had enough. Then, at last, there was a quiet rumble from Haggis.

'One . . .' Haggis began.

There was a long pause.

'Two . . . three . . .'

Another pause.

61

'Four . . . five . . . six . . . seven
. . . nine . . . ten!'

'Wait, wait!' I heard Dad cry. 'Just
say that again?'

Haggis repeated, more confidently
this time, 'One, two, three, four, five,
six, seven, nine, ten!'

'What about eight?' wailed Dad.
'The number eight!' Aw, Haggis.
So close.

'ARRGGHH!'

yelled Dad hysterically. 'This is exactly
why we had to stop with Eddie!'

Well, what did he expect? I had
to find some way to make him stop,
didn't I?

I tried to tune out Dad's moaning
and listen to the voices coming
from the kitchen instead. I wondered
if Mum and Fiend were getting along
any better . . .

A Lesson for Fiend
(continued)

'Right. So. Shapes,' said Mum. She
sounded a little weary. 'Let's try again.
This piece of cheese is a *tri-an-gle*.'
There was a pause. Then I heard the
unmistakable sound of Fiend chomping
on something greedily.

'Ri-an-gle!' he mumbled with his
mouth full. 'Mmmm!' There was a
gulping noise as he swallowed the
cheese, followed by a loud monster
burp. Nice.

'Good!' cried Mum. 'Now this
block of butter is a *rectangle*.'

Mum was obviously resorting

to bribery to try to teach Fiend the basic shapes. A sort of food-based brainwashing. It seemed she had no shame either.

There were more gobbling sounds and another belch. 'Mmmm!' cried Fiend.

'Rectangle! Mm-mm-mmmm!'

'Now,' said Mum. 'This is a hard one. This tomato is a *sphere*.'

Fiend clearly thought he had this nailed. 'Ship it in! Aahhh!' he yelled. 'Yummy sphere! Ha ha!'

A few moments later, there was a sudden, very loud growling sound. I recognized it as one of Fiend's impressive monster tummy-rumbles.

'Was that your stomach?' said Mum. 'Wow! I thought a plane was in trouble!'

'Erm,' said Fiend sheepishly. 'Is it just me or did you say that sphere was kind of . . . tomato-y?'

'It was a tomato,' confirmed Mum. 'You've had about ten.'

'Ah. Yes,' agreed Fiend. 'It's just that . . . well . . . I'm sort of allergic to tomatoes.'

Uh-oh.

'Allergic how?' said Mum, sounding worried.

'Oh, nothing serious,' said Fiend. 'A mild rash. A little headache. And er . . . some parts of my body might . . . explode just a teensy bit.'

The gurgling, growling, rumbling
noises were getting louder now.

'Er, you might want to take cover!'
said Fiend.

A moment later, there was the
sound of a very sticky **EXPLOSION**.
It was followed by a few seconds of
silence. Then I heard Fiend's cheerful
voice again.

'I think I'm going to call *that* shape
a *splatoid*!'

Mission Failure

I'm not sure what happened next.
I must have fallen asleep. I'd been
getting more and more sleepy as I was
listening to the disastrous lessons. The
last thing I remembered was hearing
about Fiend's splatoid. The next thing
I knew, it was morning. Dad was
standing over me, looking more than
a little puzzled as to why I was there –
on the doormat.

'Morning, son,' he said sleepily.
He was still wearing his ridiculous red
dungarees. And he looked exhausted.
But what really hit me was what he had
in his hand.

I blinked and woke up fast. Dad

was holding the morning's post. He must have just collected it. It had arrived while I was still asleep. And among the bunch of envelopes Dad was clutching I could see one with my school logo on it. My report.

Dad yawned, turned and staggered towards the kitchen. If he followed his usual morning routine, he'd fix himself a cup of coffee and open the post while he drank it.

Which meant I was dead.

I was staring after Dad, lost in panic, when Fiend and Haggis came bumbling into the hall. They looked nearly as tired as Dad. Haggis was shuffling along, mumbling numbers to himself.

'One, two, three, four, five, six, seven, nine, ten!' Fiend was moving like a zombie, too.

'Dad's got the report!' I hissed at them. 'Everything's gone pear-shaped!'

Fiend looked at me. 'Pear-shaped?' he muttered in a fluster. 'Wait, I know this one . . .'

I had a feeling that Fiend had spent the night learning the shapes of everything edible in our kitchen. But now wasn't the time to test his knowledge. Somehow, we *had* to stop Dad opening my report.

'Listen!' I whispered to Fiend and Haggis. 'If you ever want to hang out with me again, then we need a genius idea. *Right now!*' They both grunted, nodded, then looked completely lost.

'Or a **DUMB** idea will do fine!' I added. After all, I was desperate.

The Dumb Idea

I pressed up against the kitchen door, peeking through the crack. I had my fingers crossed. Fiend's plan was a bit too . . . well . . . 'Fiend-style' for my liking. I wasn't at all sure it would work. But it was too late for second thoughts. Through the door, I could make out the sound of Dad pouring coffee for himself and Mum.

'Well, at least the post arrived today,' I heard Dad say sleepily. Mum grunted in reply. They both sounded really groggy. A moment later, I heard Haggis and Fiend charge up to the kitchen table to surprise my parents.

'**PRESENTS!**' shrieked Fiend cheerfully.

'Heh! What the –' started Dad. But whatever he said next was drowned out by the noise of Haggis emptying a crate of apples all over the kitchen table.

'**PRESENTS!**' boomed Haggis. 'Because now you're like our *teachers* and we *have* to give you presents!'

'**Yeah!**' yelled Fiend, as if this was
a logical explanation and should be
obvious. 'Just a little thank-you present
from your favourite students!'

Outside the door, I tensed. I was
waiting for the inevitable explosion
from Mum and Dad. But amazingly,
there wasn't a peep from them. Just
stunned silence. Sometimes, the guys
leave my folks lost for words. Now
that's a skill I wish I could learn.

While my parents were staring at
the apples rolling around on the table,
and working out what to say, Fiend
whipped my report from the pile of
post without either of them noticing.
He whizzed it under the door to me.
SUCCESS!

I grabbed the envelope and hurried away from the door. As I passed the stairs, I allowed myself a little victory celebration. I punched the air with relief. *Yes!* But my feeling of triumph didn't last long.

In a cruel twist of fate, my sister was on the stairs right at that moment. Quick as a flash, she reached over the banister and snatched the envelope from me. Like all evil creatures, she can strike with inhuman speed.

Just when it seemed I was out of danger, my report had once again fallen into enemy hands.

Sister of No Mercy

'HEY! THAT'S MINE!'

Angela wasn't about to hand the envelope back, despite my protests. Instead, she gave me a smug grin, tore the envelope open and took out the dreaded report. As she flicked through it, her eyes lit up with delight. It must have been as bad as I'd feared.

'Wow!' said Angela. 'I haven't seen *this* many F's in print since I added Effy Faffelfoffy in my phone!' Ha ha. Very funny. Not.

My sister was loving this. She knew that report had the power to

get me grounded for life. There was
nothing for me to do but beg.

'All right, Angela.' The words
stuck in my throat. 'What do I have to
do to stop you showing that to Mum
and Dad?'

My sister looked like I'd just
offered her an open box of chocolates.
'Hmmm . . .' She took her time,
enjoying every moment. I'd get her
back for this. 'Say, "Eddie is rubbish
at everything and Angela is the
greatest."'

I took a deep breath and tried
to swallow my pride. Think about the
report, Eddie . . . 'Eddie is rubbish at
everything,' I mumbled, 'and Angela is
the greatest.' My sister beamed smugly.

'But she's not very original when it comes to giving out orders,' I muttered, scowling at her. Angela's eyes flashed. She wasn't going to let me get away with that.

'All right then,' she said. 'Promise never to do that thing when you open your mouth while you're eating, just to bug me.' She glared at me.

'EVER AGAIN.'

Argh! She couldn't be serious, surely? Did she have absolutely *no* mercy? I *live* for those gross-out-your-sister moments . . .

'Well?' Angela waved my report at me threateningly. 'Promise, Eddie. Or else . . .'

I knew I had to stop her handing it over. And I *tried* to make the necessary sacrifice, honestly. But there are some things too sacred to surrender. Sometimes, you have to make a stand.

'You ask the **impossible**,' I told her flatly.

Angela raised her eyebrows. 'So be it!' She marched down the stairs and made straight for the kitchen door, keeping my report well out of reach as she pushed past.

That was it then. She was going to give it to my parents. I was history.

The Heat is On

Mum and Dad were still in the kitchen
with Fiend and Haggis, clearing up
the monsters' surprise 'present', when
Angela and I burst into the kitchen.
Angela had my report behind her
back. For the time being, she was
hiding it from my parents.

'Mum, Dad – *Eddie* has something
to tell you.' I've never seen my sister
so chirpy. She *loves* watching me get
toasted.

'It's about his school report,'
Angela went on. 'There's a very good
reason why you haven't seen it yet.'

Dad gave her a puzzled look, then turned to me. 'There is?'

Mum looked at me, too. 'Well, Eddie?'

I felt like a rabbit in the headlights. My mind went blank with fear. Totally.

'Ah . . . um . . .' I began. Still nothing doing in the brain department. Zero. Nada. Zilch.

'Yeah . . . the really good reason you haven't seen it,' I said slowly, 'is because . . .' Come on, Eddie! *Think!* 'It's because . . . um . . .'

Fiend came to my rescue. Sort of. 'Because the school has been overrun with hideous giant mutant hamsters!' he shrieked. 'They've ripped up *all* the school reports to make a big evil

hamster nest-lair, from where they plot our **DooM!**' Mum and Dad stared at Fiend. 'What?' he muttered, looking hurt that no one believed him. 'That could happen.'

If I was to have even the slightest chance of blagging my way out of this, I needed to come up with something fast. Before Fiend blew my credibility completely.

'No, no, no,' I told my parents hurriedly. 'The real reason you haven't seen my report is because . . . they're

not going to send it in the post at all!'
My mind raced. 'You know . . . to save
on paper? So . . . they're going to . . .
telephone you!'

There. Not brilliant, but possible.
Even believable, maybe.

Dad looked doubtful. 'When?'
he asked.

'Tonight?' I tried.

'Oh.' Dad looked at Mum for a
moment, then shrugged. 'OK.'

'It makes sense,' agreed Mum.

Yes! I'd bought myself a little time.
They'd both gone for my story.

'Mine was better,' grumbled Fiend.

I was too busy heading for the
door to argue. When you can't stand
the heat, there's only one thing to do.

Get out of the kitchen.

As I pushed past my sister into the hall, Angela gave me a sly grin. She was still having fun. 'I can't wait to see how you get out of *this* one, Eddie,' she said quietly.

Nor could I.

Who's a Doofus?

'How could I be so stupid?'

The guys watched me with anxious looks as I banged my head on my bedroom desk in frustration. Fiend was probably worried my brain was going to explode again. It might as well, for all the use it was.

I'd just about got away with my on-the-spot excuse in the kitchen, but I'd only set myself up for another major headache. Now my parents were expecting a telephone call from school. A call that wouldn't happen.

'Oh, come on, Eddie!' said Fiend supportively. *'You're* not stupid!'

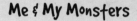

'No?'

Fiend shook his head. 'Remember the time you sailed round the world single-handed?'

What? I'd never sailed anywhere. What was he talking about? Then the penny dropped.

'That was a kid on TV!' I told him. 'I watched it with you.'

'Oh.' Fiend seemed unconvinced. 'It *looked* like you . . .'

'It was a *girl*!' I pointed out. Thanks a lot, Fiend.

'Oh, well,' he said, obviously disappointed. 'Maybe you *are* a doofus.'

Or am I? An idea had just popped into my head that made me think I might not be a total numbskull after all.

'Norman?'

'BA-DING-GLING?'

'Are you up for
a little mission behind
enemy lines?' I asked.

'Bo-Bo!'

confirmed Norman
enthusiastically. **'PRRRIILLLLLING!'**

Right then. Game on.

Phoney Phone Call

Norman had no trouble snaffling
Angela's mobile phone from her
room. He's had a *lot* of practice at
pinching stuff. And since my sister had
helped get me into this mess, it was
only fair I used her phone to help get
me out of it.

I dialled the number of our house
phone on Angela's mobile, then quickly
passed it to Fiend, who was sitting
on my bed next to me. Haggis and
Norman crowded round, listening
anxiously. I heard the phone ring
a couple of times. Then my dad's
voice came over the mobile's tiny

loudspeaker. I could just make out what he was saying.

'Hello. Carlson residence.'

We were on. I nudged Fiend and silently signalled for him to reply. I mustn't let Dad hear me in the background.

'Uh, hello,' said Fiend in a fake, high-pitched voice. 'This is Fiend talking.'

Not a great start. He was supposed to be pretending to be my teacher! I glared at him and shook my head.

'No-no-no! *Sorry!*' shrieked Fiend.

'This is *Miss Fee* calling. From Eddie's *school*.'

I only hoped he was going to get more convincing as he went along. So far, even my dad wasn't likely to be taken in. And that was saying something. Fortunately, Dad seemed to be buying it. At least for now.

'Ah, yes!' I heard him say. 'Um . . . can you hold on for one second? My wife's here, too. I'm going to put you on speaker.' There was a brief silence, then his voice came again.

'*Miss Fee*?' He sounded a bit puzzled. Which wasn't surprising, since I'd never had a teacher called that. 'Are you new?' Fiend looked at me for guidance. I nodded energetically.

'Ah, yes! That's right. I'm on exchange,' Fiend told Dad. 'Errrm . . . from Ant World.'

I cringed. If he kept adding his own details, we were in trouble. But Dad didn't seem to notice anything odd. It was Mum's voice that came over the phone next.

'Miss Fee, is this about Eddie?'

'No, no . . . I don't know any Eddie,' Fiend replied cunningly. 'It's only me here.' And he calls *me* a doofus! I shook my head wildly again.

'Oh, oh, *yes!*' Fiend quickly corrected himself. '*Yes!* This *is* about Eddie! Yes. I'm calling to talk to you about his report from the school.'

Better. Much better.

'*Yes*, from the *school*,' Fiend continued. 'Where *I* am. On the phone.' He paused, then added, 'I *like* the phone. It is *shiny*.'

Oh, dear.

'That's . . . nice,' said Dad's tinny voice. 'So – how is Eddie doing at school?'

I gave him a clear double thumbs-up sign, so he'd answer 'really good'.

'Erm . . . Eddie . . .' Fiend was staring at me, looking confused. 'Eddie . . . has . . . *beautiful thumbs*!'

What? Honestly, I give up.

'*Pardon?*' said Mum. Finally, Fiend's monster brain got there.

'No-no!' he shrieked in his Miss

Fee voice. 'I mean Eddie . . . errr . . . Eddie is . . . Eddie is *good*! *Yes!* He is *very* clever. Yes, yes . . .

Eddie is the best at EVERYTHING!'

Phew. That was more like it.

'Really?' Dad sounded surprised. 'Are you sure?'

It's nice when parents have such confidence in their child.

'Oh, yes! Yes-yes-yes!' said Fiend. He was getting into the swing of it now. 'He's the best human that we have ever learned in school!' he raved. 'In fact, I think you should *reward* him. I don't know, er, maybe build him a

93

nice mud bath in the basement, for example. Hmmmn?'

Uh-oh. I was frantically gesturing at him to wrap it up. He looked confused again.

'Oh, sorry! Er . . . I have to go now,' he said into the phone. 'I'm . . .' I did the sign for 'cut', the old hand chop across the throat gesture.

'. . . *dying?*' Fiend tried.

Take it from me – if you're going for subtlety, never work with monsters.

Saint Agony's

As it turned out, the phone conversation wasn't over. Because my parents had something they wanted to talk about.

'The thing is, Miss Fee,' I heard my mum's faint voice say, 'we've not been happy with Eddie's schooling for some time.'

This was news to me. I thought they quite rated my school. And I'd only been there since we moved back to England.

'Yeah,' Dad agreed. 'We haven't told him this yet, but we've decided to send him away to a boarding school. On a remote island.'

Boarding school? Remote island? My heart suddenly started beating much more quickly.

'Saint Agony's School for Wayward Boys,' said Mum. 'We've heard it's very good.'

'What?' I said out loud – then clamped my hand over my mouth, remembering I wasn't meant to be there. It was supposed to be just 'Miss Fee' calling from the school. Fiend saw that I was rattled. He panicked and decided to abort the call.

'Erm . . . good idea!' he shrieked into the handset. 'OK, then! *Bye bye!*' He hung up and tossed Angela's phone over his shoulder to Haggis, who swallowed it.

'Remind me to clean that before
we put it back in Angela's room,' Fiend
muttered.

Haggis looked as shocked as I
was feeling. 'What did they mean,
Eddie?' he rumbled. 'Are you *really*
going to *leave* us?'

Norman let out a despairing hoot.

I didn't know what to say.

97

I couldn't believe my parents had arranged for me to go to boarding school. Without even talking to me about it. Even for grown-ups that stunk.

'They can't do that, can they?' Fiend said. 'I mean, if you're not here, who will play with *us*? Who will make fun of human dad-thingy with us?' A look of utter panic crossed his face.

'Who will bring us cheese crackers?'

'Ooohh!' Haggis, too, looked horror-struck. 'Tell us, Eddie!' he urged me. 'How do we get out of *this* one?'

I didn't reply for a moment or two. The terrible truth was still sinking in. For once, there was no clever scheme to

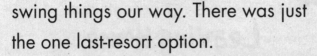

swing things our way. There was just
the one last-resort option.

'There's only one thing we can do
this time, boys,' I told the three of them
gravely. My heart felt heavy just at the
thought of it. I looked up sadly into
their anxious monster faces.

'Run.'

Leaving Home

There was no time to lose. If Mum and Dad were planning to ship me off to some remote island, the sooner we made a run for it, the better.

I told the guys to gather up their essential belongings, then hurried to my room to do the same. When I was ready, I sneaked down into the hall – just as they appeared through the door to their basement den.

'This is it, boys,' I whispered to them grimly. 'Either we leave now or it's Saint Agony's for me and home alone with Angela for you. So – keep it nice and quiet.'

It suddenly struck me what a massive amount of stuff they had with them. 'Hang on, I thought we said just the essentials?'

'What?' said Fiend, as if I was being unreasonable. 'We left behind Norman's favourite wall . . .'

Norman let out a small wailing sound. He was obviously a bit upset about this.

There wasn't much point in arguing.
I signalled for them to follow me to the
front door. But Fiend wasn't ready to go.

'Are you sure about this, Eddie?' he
asked. 'I mean, we've only ever been
outside once before. And that didn't turn
out so well.' A haunted look came over
his face. He looked up at Haggis and
Norman. 'Remember . . . *The Incident?*'

All three of them suddenly looked
paralysed by fear. They stared ahead,
wide-eyed, with glazed expressions.
It looked like they were reliving some
dreadful memory. Haggis let out a
terrified moan. I'd never seen them like
this. I made a mental note to ask them
more about this 'Incident' another day.
But right now, there was no time.

'Snap out of it!' I hissed.

Suddenly, they were back with me.
Fiend shook his head. 'Brrrrr, sorry!
Flashback!'

I signalled for them to follow me again.
'Come on! And keep it down.' I was
wasting my breath. Haggis had hardly
taken a step before he made a very
loud, very rude noise.

'Ooh!' He gave me an embarrassed grin. 'Sorry about that!'

'Ssshhhh!'

But I needn't have bothered. We hadn't even made it to the front door when it suddenly swung open. Mum and Dad stepped into the hall from outside and blocked our path.

'Evening all!' said Dad. He gave me one of those smug smiles grown-ups do when they've caught you red-handed. Mum looked pretty pleased with herself, too. My heart sank even further as I saw why. She was holding up a sheet of paper.

'Special delivery!' beamed Mum. It was a copy of my school report.

The Big Scam

I looked at Mum and Dad, leaning against the kitchen worktop. I'd never seen them smugger. Dad, in particular, was looking very pleased with himself.

Me and the guys were squashed up on the kitchen sofa. It's where I often end up listening to a lecture from my parents, when I'm in trouble.

'So there never was a Saint Agony's School for Wayward Boys?' I asked Mum.

'Nope,' she replied, smirking.

The whole boarding school thing had been a set-up. And I'd fallen for it, like a complete sucker. Dad was grinning like an idiot. He was so chuffed they had tricked me. He started doing a little victory dance.

'We got you! We got you!' he chanted. Remind me – which one of us is supposed to be the grown-up? I tried to ignore him and talked to Mum instead.

'And you had my school report all along?'

Mum nodded. 'They emailed it to us days ago.' She gave me a wicked smile. 'So we thought we'd teach you the kind of lesson you don't get in school.'

Dad was still milking it. He mimed casting a fishing line, then landing a catch. 'Reeeeeled in!' he taunted me. '*Rrrrrrrrrrr!* Hook, line and sinker!'

OK, Dad. Enough already. But he wasn't done yet. He made an L-sign against his forehead with his finger and thumb.

'Loser!' he crowed. 'Loser!'

Mum gave him a look. 'You *might* be undermining the message about *maturity* that we're trying to impart here,' she told Dad.

Dad tried to look a little more serious. 'Oh. Right. OK.' He struggled to get his grin under control. 'Fire away.'

Mum turned her attention back
to me. She held up my report. 'So,
Eddie,' she began with a stern face.

Here it came. Toasting time. I
braced myself.

Good News (Mostly)

'It turns out your report isn't as bad as you feared.'

I nearly fell off the sofa. Mum smiled at my shocked reaction. She tossed the report over to me, then watched, arms folded, as I quickly skimmed through it. I could hardly believe it. It was *way* better than I'd expected.

'Is that an A in creative writing?'

It was a good job I was sitting down. I *never* got A grades. I read out my teacher's comment, stunned.

'"Eddie is to be commended on his vivid monster stories"!' Fiend, Haggis

and Norman let out approving noises.
I looked across at Mum in delighted
disbelief. She was smiling, too.

'**"Disturbingly vivid"**, if I recall
correctly,' she said. 'But we're very
proud of you.' She quickly put on her
serious face again. 'Although you *are*
still grounded.'

Rats. There wasn't any point in
protesting, though.

'Interfering with the mail is a
criminal offence after all, son,' said
my dad solemnly. Then he added in a
whisper, behind the back of his hand,
'We *got* you!'

'All right, all right. Well done,'
I said grudgingly. 'Nice scam.'

Dad shrugged smugly. 'What can I

110

A A A

say? When you've got it, you've *got* it.'

Mum pulled a face. 'And *you're*
going to take all the credit, are you?'
she asked. 'Like it was all *your* idea?'

They were *still* fighting over who
was the smartest. I could see that this
was going to run and run. Unless there
was a way they could settle it once
and for all . . .

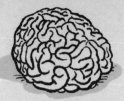

The Moment of Truth

This was it. Show time. Whichever of my parents could prove that they had taught their monster student the most would be crowned smartest Carlson grown-up. Mum and Fiend were up first. Dad and Haggis watched nervously.

'OK, Fiend.' Mum let out a deep breath. 'Let's show them what you've got.' She held up a big red tomato. 'What *shape* is this?'

Fiend fixed his many eyes on it, concentrating hard. 'Ah . . . er . . . um . . .'

I could almost hear his monster

brain straining for the right answer. But a moment later, his head slumped and he let out a sigh of defeat.

'I'm not sure,' he said dejectedly. Then he cheered up a bit. 'But I could turn it into a **SPLATOID** if you like?'

Mum let out a disappointed sigh. 'He's much better at geography,' she told Dad. But Dad was already gloating.

'Hah! Step aside, dunces!' he told Mum and Fiend. 'My star pupil, Haggis, will count to ten! Do your thing, Hag!'

Haggis stepped forward to take centre stage. 'Ah . . . ooohh . . .' he mumbled, looking terrified.

'He gets a little nervous,' Dad explained casually. He gave Haggis an encouraging nod.

'Umm . . . one . . .' began Haggis, using every part of his tiny monster brain to concentrate. 'Two . . . three . . .'

Impressive stuff so far.

'Four . . . five . . . six . . . seven . . .'

Haggis paused and I saw Dad clench his fists in suspense.

'. . . EIGHT!'

Dad let out a 'Yes!' of triumph. He thought they were home and dry now. But Haggis was so relieved to have made it to eight that he got overexcited. He lost it completely. Instead of the easy 'nine, ten' finish Dad was expecting, Haggis went freestyle.

'**EIGHT!**' he boomed confidently. '**EIGHT! Eight-eight-eight! Eight! Eight-eight! Eight! Eight-eight-eight-eight-eight-eight-eight! Eight!**'

As Haggis ran around the room,
Dad put his head in his hands. Mum
patted him on the shoulder sportingly.
'Call it a draw?' she suggested.

Dad nodded. His will to teach,
and to compete, was all used up.
'Yup,' he agreed flatly. 'Absolutely.'

Monster Smart

So – there you have it. Neither Mum
nor Dad managed to prove their
own cleverness by helping Fiend and
Haggis get smarter. I guess we'll never
find out which of them Angela gets her
mega-brains from.

Although I think we all know it
isn't Dad.

Anyway, I guess when it comes
down to it, there are different *kinds*
of smart. There's Angela smart. That's
the kind that most grown-ups bang on
about. The straight-A's-in-school, fab-at-
exams, top-of-the-class kind.

Then there's Eddie smart. That's
the kind of instinct that gets me out of
tight spots. Like the plan I came up
with to return Angela's phone without
her knowing I'd had it. I flashed her
a mouthful of my half-chewed cereal
at breakfast. I knew she'd look away
in disgust – which gave me just long
enough to slip the phone into her
schoolbag without her noticing.

And then there's
a totally different kind
of smart again. The
kind that means you
can burp your favourite
TV theme tunes – like
Fiend can. Or live perfectly happily
despite being unable
to count your own
fingers – like Haggis.
Or even be able
to solve Angela's
toughest maths

homework in seconds,
while at the same time
believing a toaster is a
perfectly normal choice
of pet – like Norman.

And *that* kind of smart, if you ask me, is the best kind of all . . .

Monster smart.

Meet the Monsters

FIEND

Noisy! Never stops talking

full of (bad) ideas and advice

Boss of the monsters – because he says so!

NORMAN

Big sticky-out nose

Makes weird noises - that's just how he speaks

He's not crazy he just seems that way.

HAGGIS

Whopping monster body

Scares very easily

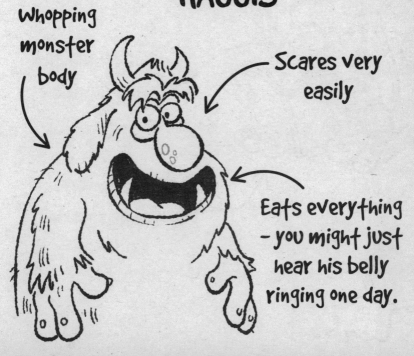

Eats everything - you might just hear his belly ringing one day.

It all started with a Scarecrow.

Puffin is seventy years old.

Sounds ancient, doesn't it? But Puffin has never been
so lively. We're always on the lookout for the next big
idea, which is how it began all those years ago.

Penguin Books was a big idea from the mind of
a man called Allen Lane, who in 1935 invented
the quality paperback and changed the world.

**And from great Penguins, great Puffins grew,
changing the face of children's books forever.**

The first four Puffin Picture Books were hatched in 1940 and the
first Puffin story book featured a man with broomstick arms called
Worzel Gummidge. In 1967 Kaye Webb, Puffin Editor, started the
Puffin Club, promising to **'make children into readers'**.
She kept that promise and over 200,000 children became
devoted Puffineers through their quarterly instalments of
Puffin Post, which is now back for a new generation.

Many years from now, we hope you'll look back and
remember Puffin with a smile. **No matter what your age
or what you're into, there's a Puffin for everyone.**
The possibilities are endless, but one thing is for sure:
whether it's a picture book or a paperback, a sticker book
or a hardback, **if it's got that little Puffin
on it – it's bound to be good.**